Paige

This book belongs to

LOOK BEFORE YOU LEAP!

Disney's

READ and GROW LIBRARY

Published by Advance Publishers
Winter Park, Florida

Written by Marc Gave   Edited by Bonnie Brook
Penciled by Edwards Artistic Services   Painted by Brad McMahon
Designed by Design Five
Cover art by Peter Emslie
Cover design by Irene Yap

ISBN: 1-885222-85-8

10 9 8 7 6 5 4 3 2 1

Morty and Ferdie were excited and happy. Uncle Mickey and Aunt Minnie had promised to take them camping and to an amusement park for a summer vacation.

Early one morning they packed all their gear in Mickey's van—a tent and sleeping bags, clothes, baseball gloves, and even fishing poles.

Luckily after they had finished, there was still room for Morty and Ferdie, so they climbed in.

"Are you ready?" Mickey called to his nephews.

"Yes, Uncle Mickey," said Morty. "Our seat belts are all buckled up."

"Then we're off on our vacation!" shouted Mickey happily. "Let's make it a fun one—and a safe one!"

They hadn't gone far when they saw someone standing in the middle of the street in front of them.

"Goofy!" shouted Mickey. "What are you doing? It's dangerous to stand in the street. You could get hurt!"

"Gawrsh, Mickey," said Goofy. "I guess you're right. But I didn't want you to forget to take me with you."

"Oh, Goofy," said Minnie. "How could we forget you? Besides, we would have seen you on the sidewalk. It's much safer there."

"You're right!" Goofy answered. "I'll remember next time."

Mickey drove out of the city and along country roads. It was a beautiful day, and the air was warm and sweet.

Morty and Ferdie were playing a travel game. They had to see how many things from their game book they could spot on their trip.

Suddenly Ferdie noticed that Pluto had stuck his head out the window.

"Whoa, boy!" shouted Ferdie. "That's not a good idea. You don't want to bump into anything out there, and you don't want anything bumping into you."

He helped Pluto pull his head back inside the van.

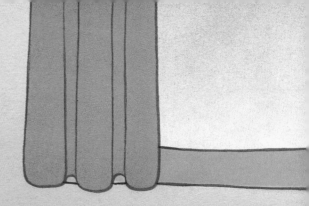

Before long the travelers stopped for lunch at a roadside restaurant. As soon as they sat down at the table, Goofy tied his napkin around his neck and stretched his leg out into the aisle.

At that very moment, the waitress came by with a tray loaded with food. Sure enough, she tripped over Goofy's foot. Food went flying everywhere.

"Don't you know it's not safe to stick your foot out in the aisle?" scolded the waitress.

"Gawrsh," said Goofy. "I'm sorry. I won't do it again— I promise."

Morty and Ferdie were done with their lunch first. While the others finished eating, they went outside and got their baseball and gloves. They had fun tossing the ball back and forth. Pluto had fun running back and forth trying to get it from them.

Then Morty threw the ball too far. It hit a rock on the ground and rolled into the road.

Pluto began to run after it.

"Stop, Pluto!" shouted Ferdie. He knew it was important to look both ways before going out into the street. After he had checked to make sure there were no cars coming, Ferdie let Pluto fetch the ball.

Soon the travelers were on the road again. It wasn't long before they reached the campsite where they were going to spend the next few days. There were deep, piney woods and a crystal-clear lake nearby.

Morty and Ferdie helped put up the tent among the tall trees. Then Minnie said she would take the boys on a hike before supper.

"Stay close by," Minnie told Pluto. She didn't want him to get lost in the woods.

After their hike, Morty and Ferdie helped gather wood for a campfire. Soon the fire was blazing safely—in an open area away from the trees.

"Mmm," said Morty. "I love hot dogs."

"Me, too," said Ferdie. "And I'm glad these long sticks keep our sleeves far away from the fire, the same way the handles on our pots and pans protect us from the stove."

Suddenly, Pluto came bounding up.

"It looks as if somebody else likes hot dogs," said Morty.

"Watch out, Pluto," said Ferdie. "Don't go too close to the fire." He gave Pluto a hot dog after it had cooled off.

The next day was sunny and hot. Everyone went down to the lake for a swim.

"Last one in is a rotten egg," called Goofy.

"No thanks, Goofy. Minnie and I are going to lie on the beach, instead," said Mickey. "That's why we're putting on sunscreen—to protect ourselves from getting sunburned."

Meanwhile Morty, Ferdie, and Pluto walked along the shore to where a cliff overhung the lake. Pluto trotted to the edge and got ready to jump off into the water.

"Stop, Pluto!" shouted Morty. "Always look before you leap. The sign says, 'No diving. Rocks below.' It's not safe to dive or even swim here."

NO DIVING
ROCKS BELOW

Pluto walked with Morty and Ferdie back to the sandy beach. Then they waded into the lake. The water was cool and clear.

Morty and Ferdie loved to swim and were good swimmers. Even so, neither of them ever went into the water alone. Each was always the other's swimming buddy. Just like on a field trip at school, each boy knew that a buddy would help him stay safe.

After lunch Morty and Ferdie decided to take a rowboat out on the water. They brought Pluto along. Before they got into the boat, the boys put on their life jackets. Even though they were good swimmers, they made sure they were extra safe. They even put a life jacket on Pluto.

The boys took turns rowing. Soon the beach was just a speck of tan a long distance away.

A few minutes later, Ferdie spotted large clouds rolling in over the lake.

"I think we'd better head in," he said. "There may be a storm blowing up. We don't want to get caught out here in a storm."

The boys rowed quickly back to the shore.

Everyone left the lake and returned to the tent. Soon the sky grew dark. Lightning flashed and thunder roared. Pluto hid in a sleeping bag.

"It's not a good idea to stay under a tree during a thunderstorm," Mickey said. "Since we can't get to a house, we'll all be a lot safer sitting in the van."

Inside the van, Minnie said, "You can tell how far away a thunderstorm is, just by counting. When you see a flash of lightning, start counting the seconds—one, two, three…. If you get up to five, then the storm is a mile away."

The boys had fun trying to count how far away the storm was.

Soon the thunderstorm left completely, and the gang continued to have a great time camping for the next few days.

Finally, one morning everyone helped take down the tent and pack up the van. It was time to go to the amusement park.

Morty and Ferdie could hardly wait. They had barely arrived at the park when they saw the roller coaster. They ran up to the ride and squeezed into a seat with Pluto.

Ferdie made sure Pluto wasn't hanging over the edge. "It's just like when you ride in the van. All of you should be inside," he said.

After the roller coaster, the boys could hardly wait to
go on the ferris wheel and the carousel. But it was
hotter than it had been all week, and soon everybody
was tired and hot.

"Let's take a rest in the shade," suggested Mickey.
"We can get our energy back and drink some water.
When you sweat a lot, your body needs to get back the
water you lose. That way it can stay healthy."

Everybody had a good long drink. Mickey filled the water bottle and squirted water into Pluto's mouth. Pluto thought it was a game and had fun.

Soon Morty and Ferdie had to go to the bathroom. Mickey went with them.

On the way out he had them stop at the sink to wash their hands with soap and water.

"Washing gets rid of a lot of germs that make us sick," Mickey said.

When Mickey and the boys joined the others, it was time for lunch.

On the way to the lunch station they passed an ice-cream stand.

"We want ice cream!" Morty and Ferdie shouted.

"Fine," said Minnie. "But first you must eat your lunch. Then you can have ice cream as a treat for dessert."

After lunch Morty and Ferdie asked for super-sized cones with sprinkles.

"Sorry, boys," said Minnie, "if you eat too much ice cream, you'll get sick to your stomachs. Especially if you go on any more rides."

"And we do want to go on more rides!" the boys shouted.

"Then we'll play it safe and get you each a medium-sized cone," Minnie said.

"Let's go check out some of the other rides," suggested Morty after they had finished their ice cream.

"Great," said Ferdie.

The boys and Pluto began to wander through the crowd.

Suddenly they stopped. They realized they were lost. They needed to find their way back to Mickey, Minnie and Goofy as quickly as possible.

But they had no idea which way to go.

Suddenly, someone they didn't know walked up to them. "Hey, boys," he said, "your folks asked me to come get you."

Morty and Ferdie didn't believe him for a second. Mickey and Minnie didn't even know where the boys were, so how could they send this stranger? And besides, if they knew, why didn't they just come for the boys themselves? Most of all, the boys knew they should never go anywhere with someone they didn't know.

So they refused to go with him. And when Pluto showed his teeth, the stranger left in a hurry.

Soon Morty and Ferdie saw a booth marked "Information." When they got there, Mickey, Minnie, and Goofy were waiting for them, looking worried. Minnie gave each of the boys a big hug, and they told her what had happened.

"You know you did something very unsafe," she scolded. "I don't want you ever to do it again. When you get older and start going places by yourselves, it's important always to know where you are. As you pass different places, try to remember as many of them as you can and the order in which you passed them. And boys," Minnie concluded, "it's never too early to practice."

Finally it was time to leave the park.

On the ride home, Morty and Ferdie fell asleep. They woke up just as the van stopped in front of Goofy's house.

"So long," shouted Goofy. "Thanks for everything. I had a great vacation." He waved wildly as he walked backward toward his front steps.

"Goofy, watch out!" shouted Minnie.

But it was too late. Goofy tripped over a skateboard he had left in the yard. Goofy and the skateboard went flying in different directions. They landed—thud!—on the ground.

"Gawrsh," said Goofy. "I guess they're right when they say most accidents happen at home. I'm going to try to be a lot safer."

Pluto barked in agreement.